Mummy Time

Judith Kerr

HarperCollins *Children's Books*

First published in hardback in Great Britain
by HarperCollins Children's Books in 2018

10 9 8 7 6 5 4 3 2 1

ISBN: 978-0-00-830680–9

HarperCollins Children's Books is a division of HarperCollins Publishers Ltd.

Text and illustrations copyright © Kerr-Kneale Productions Ltd 2018

Visit our website at www.harpercollins.co.uk

Printed and bound in China

MIX
Paper from
responsible sources
FSC® C007454

FSC is a non-profit international organisation established to promote the
responsible management of the world's forests. Products carrying the FSC
label are independently certified to assure consumers that they come
from forests that are managed to meet the social, economic and
ecological needs of present and future generations.

Find out more about HarperCollins and the environment at
www.harpercollins.co.uk/green

"…just taking the little one out
for a bit of mummy time…

…but my dear, the party last night…
some very odd faces there,
I thought…

…yes, the one with the awful teeth…

…actually he was rather sweet…

…but the food…
I know she had a lot
of mouths to feed…

…well, all I can say is, different people have different tastes…

…I suppose they wanted to make
a bit of a splash. Before this they
could barely keep their heads
above water. But they saw this
chance and grabbed it with both hands…

…and now they're riding high…

…which is not how things are with us.
Luck just seems to pass us by these days…

*…and I'm sort of used
to just hanging on…*

...and living from hand to mouth...

…but then something happens…

…and you come down to earth with a bump…

…the other day in a shop I saw this
beautiful little striped woolly which
would have been perfect for me…

… but of course I couldn't have it…

… but I really loved it…

…and I just burst into tears. It was awful.

Everyone was looking at me...

*… but, my dear, I'm sorry you've had
to listen to all this misery…*

*… I expect that sooner or later
something good will come our way again…*

*…and as long as I've got the
little one, and a friend like yourself,
I can't complain…*

*...which reminds me
I'd better go and see
where he's got to."*

"Come on then. Say goodbye to that smelly doggie, and we'll go home for tea.

We had a nice time, didn't we?"